The Legend of Blackbeard

Written by Thomas Bloor

Illustrated by Ivan Kravets

Collins

Chapter 1

"Spanish gold!" I say, and I hold up the coin.
A hush falls. I flick my thumb and up goes the little
gold disc. It spins through the smoky air, sparkling in
the lamplight. Everybody watches it. Solomon Beets,
Old Knock, Boy Galloway and all of my crew.
All my bonny lads.

The coin lands on the table, and I slam my palm
down on top of it with a mighty slap.

"One gold piece!" I cry. "One gold piece to any of you who can beat me in a swimming race, three times round the ship! Let's go, boys!" And I'm stripping off my topcoat and kicking off my sea boots before the words have left my mouth. I run for the door and out into the warm Caribbean air.

There's uproar in the cabin behind me, with all the crew shouting at once. I know what they're thinking. *Has the captain gone mad? A swimming race, here on the open sea? He'll be drowned, for sure.* I know none of them will dare race with me, but that's not the point.

3

"There's sharks in these waters,
Cap'n!" somebody calls.

"Then you'd better tell 'em to
watch out!" I shout back.
"'Cos Blackbeard the pirate
is coming in for a dip!"

A gale of laughter and a great cheer goes up at that. And this is why they follow me, why they'd go with me to the ends of the earth itself. I live loud and I live large and I'm afraid of nothing. Or at least, that's what I'd have them all believe.

I grab a rope and leap up onto the lower rungs of the rigging. Leaning forward, I swing out over the sea, feeling the breeze in my hair. I'm just about to dive into the dark blue water when a shout comes from the lookout in the crow's nest. "A sail! A sail ho!"

I freeze. All eyes are on me. I scan the horizon but see no sign of any ship.

"A spyglass!" I call, and I stretch out my hand.
Old Knock throws his brass telescope to me.
I catch it and bring it to my eye. And there,
on the horizon, I see a sail.

"All hands on deck!" I bellow. "We give chase
at once!"

"Aye, Cap'n!" the crew roar back. The ship is alive with activity as every man hurries to his post – some to the gun deck, others to the rigging. Up they go, climbing high into the masts to fix our sails ready for the chase to come.

I jump back onto the deck. Here comes Boy Galloway,
carrying my coat and boots. His arms are full.
He also has my belt, my cutlass and pistols.

"And bring me two thin candles," I tell him.
"The ones that burn with a green flame.
And the flag, Boy. Don't forget the flag."

I designed our flag myself. Solomon cut and stitched
it from a length of fine silk taken from an English
trading ship. The flag is black, with a white skeleton
and a blood-red heart. Anyone who sees that flag
knows what it means: Blackbeard is coming,
and you should be very, very afraid.

Chapter 2

✠

Our ten-gun ship is called *The Dream*. She's small and light and fast. It's not long before the vessel we spotted on the horizon is in range of our cannon.

"She's French," says Old Knock, standing beside me at the rail. His eyes are fixed on the ship we're attacking. "She's twice our size, and with three times as many guns!"

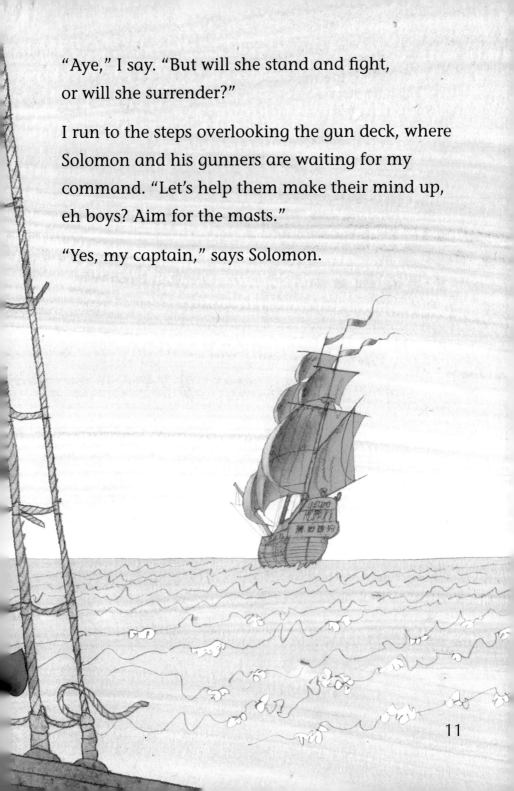

"Aye," I say. "But will she stand and fight,
or will she surrender?"

I run to the steps overlooking the gun deck, where
Solomon and his gunners are waiting for my
command. "Let's help them make their mind up,
eh boys? Aim for the masts."

"Yes, my captain," says Solomon.

The cannons fire, splitting the air with thunder.
Black smoke from our guns drifts in front of the French
ship like a billowing curtain. For a moment,
we can see nothing.

I draw my cutlass. "Boy Galloway?" I say, without
looking round.

"Here, Cap'n," says Boy.

"Do you have those candles I asked for?"

"Aye, Cap'n."

"Light them, Boy, then hand them to me."

Boy does as I ask. I push the unlit ends of the candles into my long, plaited beard. The candles flicker and spit, casting their green light over my features.

"How do I look, Boy?"

"Truly terrifying, Cap'n."

"Good," I say.

But the smoke from our guns is still hiding the French ship from view. What are they doing over there? Are they loading their cannons, preparing to fire?

I know what I must do. I jump up onto the ship's rail and stand with my sword raised above my head. So when the smoke finally clears, the first thing the French sailors will
see is me.

At last the smoke lifts. The French vessel towers over us. Our attack has shredded her sails and split her foremast. But her gun ports are all open and I stare at the rows of cannons, their black mouths gaping. Then I look up and see the men on her decks. They're armed with swords and pistols and muskets. And they're all looking at me.

There's a dreadful silence. All that can be heard is the slap of the waves against the hull, and the creaking of the ship's timbers. And then …

"Allow me to introduce myself," I call out. "You might have heard of me. I am Blackbeard!"

Almost at once, there's a clatter from the deck of the French ship. A man in a powdered wig and a velvet coat has thrown down his sword: their captain.

"They're surrendering!" cries Old Knock.

All my crew are cheering. I give a grin and lift
my hat to the French captain, who glares back at me.
Boy punches the air, Old Knock dances the hornpipe
and even Solomon is smiling. We've seized the French
ship and life feels good.

Chapter 3

☠

"This ship is bigger and stronger than ours," I say to my crew. "Perhaps we should take her for ourselves, eh boys?"

"But what about *The Dream*?" says Knock.

"We'll set her adrift," I decide. "She can sail wherever she wants, without any crew to bother her."

So that's what we do. I have everything we need put aboard our new ship. Then we set *The Dream* loose. Wind fills her sails and away she goes – an empty ship, heading who knows where. I stand at the rail and watch her go.

When I see what's stowed below in the hold of
the French ship, I'm not so happy. She's a slaver.
The cargo she carries is human beings.
People chained up and crammed together in the
darkness below decks. When I come back into the
sunlight again, I'm angry.

"First thing we do is rename this French ship," I say.
"And since I learnt everything I know about the sea
from fighting the French in good Queen Anne's navy,
we'll call her *Queen Anne's Revenge!*"

Most of the crew nod in agreement. Some just shrug. They didn't all fight for Queen Anne.

"Next," I say, "we'll repair the sails and the foremast. And then we'll head for the nearest land and release the slaves."

"But, Cap'n," Boy Galloway pipes up, "that's valuable cargo. Shouldn't we find a port and sell the slaves for money? We're pirates, after all."

"No!" I pound my fist against the polished railing. "Nobody," I roar, "should ever make a slave of anyone! If it were me, I would rather die than live in chains!"

And so it's decided. We sail to the island of Bequia, where we put the slaves ashore. I'd expected them to celebrate their freedom, but they don't. Maybe they've suffered too much. They stand around watching us in silence, until they disappear into the forest beyond the beach, leaving in ones or twos.

"Good luck to you," I say, as I watch them go.

"And what shall we do with the French crew, Blackbeard?" asks Old Knock.

"I hate slavers," I say, and I clench my teeth. "Kill them all."

"Wait, Cap'n!" says Boy. "There aren't enough of us to sail a ship this size. The French crew will be useful. We don't have a carpenter. They do. And they've got a surgeon, and a decent cook, too."

This time, I decide to listen to Boy. "Very well," I say. "If these Frenchmen are willing to join a pirate crew, then so be it."

When I go to bed that night, the number of men under my command has more than doubled. And now I sail in a much bigger ship. But I can't sleep. I lie in the dark of my cabin and remember how *The Dream* looked as she sailed away into the distance.

Chapter 4

☠

When morning comes, the sun warms the decking and sets the sea sparkling. I dunk my head in a water barrel to wake myself up. There's not a cloud in the sky and a fair wind fills our sails. Out on the deck, Solomon is manning the wheel.

"Where to, my captain?" he asks.

I walk over to the compass, close my eyes and lay one finger gently on the dial. I open my eyes to see where my finger is pointing.

"North," I say. "Let's go north."

So we follow the great curve of the West Indies,
passing islands strung out like the beads
of a giant's necklace.

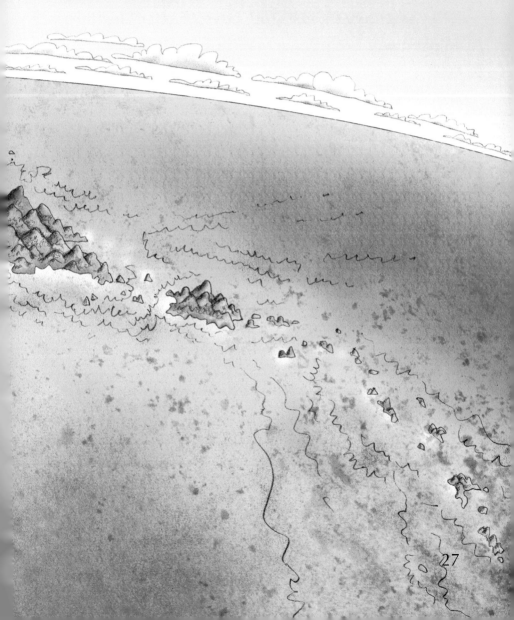

Off one of the islands, we encounter a British ship, *The Adventure*. I look through the telescope and watch her captain giving his orders. He shouts at his men, his face red with fury.

"*The Adventure*'s a fast ship, boys," I say. "She'll try to get away. We'll have to outrun her!"

I dash to the front of our ship, to the figurehead –
a huge wooden mermaid wearing a golden crown.

"Come on!" I yell as I draw my cutlass.
"Nobody escapes the *Queen Anne's Revenge*!"

We cut through the waves. Freezing spray breaks over me, soaking me to the skin. But I don't care. We're gaining on *The Adventure*. I let out a whoop of triumph. The British ship is slowing down. The chase is over. She lowers her flag in surrender.

Aboard *The Adventure,* we find the captain has been locked up by his own men.

"Our captain was a brute and a bully," one of them explains. "He ordered us to fight to the death. We decided we'd rather live."

I gather the British crew around the mainmast.

"What'll it be, lads?" I say to them. "We can lock you below decks with your captain and keep you prisoner until we're next in port. Or you can join us and live as free men."

All of them choose to join us as pirates. Now two ships fly the flag of the skeleton and the blood-red heart.

"Where to next, my captain?" asks Solomon.

"America," I say. "There's a port called Charleston, up in South Carolina. I've heard there are rich pickings there. We'll lay in wait outside the harbour. Then we'll stop any ship that approaches and make them pay us if they want to go in."

"And make them pay us again if they want to come out," adds Boy Galloway.

"Good idea, Boy," I say.

Chapter 5

Three days later, I'm getting ready for our first morning outside Charleston harbour. I'm in my cabin, plaiting my beard. Boy Galloway has gone to fetch me two thin green candles. I pick up my belt, my cutlass and my pistols. As I buckle the belt tight around my waist, I catch sight of my reflection in the looking glass that hangs over the chart table. There's been more food aboard ship since we took over the *Queen Anne's Revenge*. Richer food, too. I'm looking fat, and my skin is pale and unhealthy. Perhaps I need more fresh air. I adjust my belt and walk out onto the deck.

The first ship we stop is a merchant vessel from New England. They refuse to pay us the gold I demand.

"Don't you know who I am?" I bellow, as we move in alongside. The candles are sputtering in my beard, lighting my face a fearsome green colour.
"I am Blackbeard!"

I draw my cutlass and wave it above my head.
"Prepare to board her, boys," I shout to my crew.
"We'll take their gold by force!"

I'm standing on the ship's rail. I can hear it creaking
under my boots. I really have put on weight. Perhaps
a long, hard fight will do me good. It's all been a bit
too easy lately. But then I see them lower their flag.
They've surrendered after all. I put my cutlass back
in its scabbard and let out a sigh of disappointment.

By the time we leave Charleston, two weeks later, we've three more ships with us. And we haven't had to fight a single battle. I now command a fleet of five pirate ships and over 300 men. But I barely know most of them.

I tell Solomon to take us north, always north. And I lie in the dark of my cabin and think about our old ship *The Dream.* I imagine her sailing the ocean somewhere with her decks empty and her sails untrimmed.

Chapter 6

We're nearing the North Carolina coast when there's a cry from the lookout. "A sail. A sail ho!"

She's a small ship, only ten guns. Her cannons are rusty and uncared for and don't look like they've been fired in years.

"This one's hardly worth bothering with, is she, Cap'n?" says Boy Galloway.

Her sails are torn and her paintwork is blistered. But it's nothing that can't be put right with a bit of hard work. And there's something about the old ship that reminds me of *The Dream*.

I give the order, "Take us alongside."

Queen Anne's Revenge towers over the smaller ship.
Her decks are empty but for one old man,
alone at the wheel.

"Good day to you, sir," I say.

The old man looks up at me. "You're that pirate,
ain't ye?" he says. "The one they calls Blackbeard?"

"I am."

"Well, you can go ahead and sink this here pile of
junk of mine. I was only taking her to be scrapped,
and I'd have to pay the harbour master for
the privilege."

"You don't want your ship?" I say.

The old man shakes his head.

"What's her name?"

"*The Sea Breeze.*"

"And you really don't want her?"

"Nope. You'd be doing me a favour if you took her off my hands."

"Then consider it done," I say, and I give orders for the old man's ship to be taken in tow. I have the beginnings of an idea.

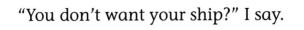

Chapter 7

A storm is gathering as the fleet follows my orders and moves in towards the shore.

Old Knock lowers his telescope. "The captains on the other ships will be wondering where we're going," he says.

"There's a little inlet nearby that'll make a perfect pirate hideout," I say.

"But aren't we getting a bit too close to the shore?"

"Don't worry," I say.

The sky has grown dark and the sails are flapping in the rising wind.

"Are you sure about this?" Old Knock looks worried.

"Oh yes," I say. "I know exactly what I'm doing."

I look out and see waves breaking on the beach. It's close enough to swim ashore. But the sea is getting rougher and rougher. The deck tips beneath our feet.

And then it happens. There's a terrible grinding sound. The ship shudders and shakes, and we come to a sudden halt. Moments later, all five ships of my pirate fleet are stuck, beached on the sandbanks in a rising storm.

The crews yell out in alarm. Around me, there's chaos aboard the *Queen Anne's Revenge* with sailors running this way and that. But I'm calm. There's a sixth ship still afloat, a ship that's much smaller than the rest. *The Sea Breeze*. Quietly, I summon my crew. Old Knock, Boy Galloway, Solomon Beets. All my bonny lads.

"Trust me," I say to them. "This is for the best. Now, follow me." And I spring over the side of the ship and scramble down a rope to our little rowing boat.

As we pull away from the *Queen Anne's Revenge*, I start to wonder if I've made a terrible mistake. Our boat is tossed on the heaving sea and spun in circles. Time and again, the waves break over us, threatening to tip us out while we cling on for dear life. But at last the wind drops and the sea grows calmer.

"We've made it, boys!" I say. We all smile with relief.

Solomon takes the oars. "Where to, my captain?" he asks.

"To *The Sea Breeze*," I say. "And then on … to the ends of the earth!"

Aboard *The Sea Breeze,* I glance over the cracked railings to where the pirate fleet lies, still stranded on the sandbank.

Boy Galloway has brought a cotton sack with him.

"What's in there, Boy?" I say.

"I saved some of your candles, Cap'n," he says. "Oh, and some gold too. It seemed a shame to leave it all behind."

"Pah!" I say. "The money doesn't matter!"

44

"I understand that, Cap'n," says Boy. "But it does come in handy sometimes."

And he reaches into the sack and takes out a single gold coin. He throws it to me, and we all watch as it spins through the air. I lift my arm and catch it in the palm of my hand.

"Spanish gold," I whisper. Then I throw off my topcoat and bellow, "Well, boys, who'll race me? Three times round the ship, and back again!"

Blackbeard's Character

☠

determined
pirate

daring
joker

happy
captain

cunning
planner

46

fierce attacker

sympathetic man

nostalgic thinker

dissatisfied victor

powerful leader

47

Ideas for reading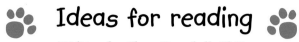

Written by Clare Dowdall, PhD
Lecturer and Primary Literacy Consultant

Reading objectives:
- discuss words and phrases that capture the reader's interest and imagination
- draw inferences and justify these with evidence
- make predictions from details stated and applied

Spoken language objectives:
- participate in discussions, presentations, performances, role play, improvisations and debates

Curriculum links: History – locational knowledge

Resources: ICT; maps of the world

Build a context for reading

- Look at the front cover and read the title. Discuss whether legends are true or false stories. Ask children to raise a list of questions about Blackbeard, based on the cover image, e.g. is he good or bad?
- Read the blurb aloud, and discuss the literal information and what can be inferred, e.g. getting what he wants doesn't make Blackbeard happy.
- Help children to make connections to the story prior to reading by discussing whether getting what they want makes them happy.

Understand and apply reading strategies

- Read pp2–5 aloud, modelling how to read expressively. Ask children who the narrator is, and what language features the author includes that help with expressive reading (special language, dialect, "pirate" phrases).
- Challenge children to describe Blackbeard, based on the information given. Discuss what can be inferred about him (he loves his crew, is full of life).